Cinderella

based on the story by Charles Perrault

retold by
Sarah L. Thomson

illustrated by
Nicoletta Ceccoli

Amazon Children's Publishing

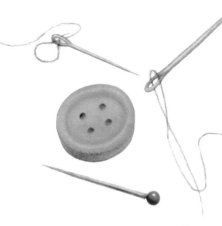

To the lovely Dalila

—N.C.

Text copyright © 2012 by Marshall Cavendish Corporation

Illustrations copyright © 2012 by Nicoletta Ceccoli

Amazon Publishing

Attn: Amazon Children's Books

P.O. Box 400818

Las Vegas, NV 89149

www.amazon.com/amazonchildrenspublishing

Library of Congress Cataloging-in-Publication Data

Thomson, Sarah L.

Cinderella / retold by Sarah L. Thomson ; illustrated by Nicoletta Ceccoli ;

based on the story by Charles Perrault. — 1st ed.

p. cm.

Summary: Although mistreated by her stepmother and stepsisters, Cinderella

meets her prince with the help of her fairy godmother.

ISBN 978-0-7614-6170-8 (hardcover) — ISBN 978-0-7614-6171-5 (ebook)

[1. Fairy tales. 2. Folklore—France.] I. Ceccoli, Nicoletta, ill. II.

Perrault, Charles, 1628-1703. Cendrillon. III. Title.

PZ8.T38Ci 2012

[Fic]—dc23

2011034873

The illustrations are rendered in acrylics on paper and digitally.

Book design by Anahid Hamparian

Editor: Robin Benjamin

Printed in China (W)

First edition

10 9 8 7 6 5 4 3 2 1

Author's Note

THIS STORY OF CINDERELLA is based on the version collected and published by the French author Charles Perrault, who was born in the seventeenth century. Perrault's *Cinderella* echoes the elegance and luxury of the French court of King Louis XIV, and it's from his version that we get Cinderella's famous glass slippers.

Perrault's story does not have the darker ending some readers may remember from another famous version, collected by the Brothers Grimm, in which Cinderella's stepsisters are punished for their cruel treatment of Cinderella. My retelling stays close to Perrault's version, but it does add one detail that is closer to the Grimm story—the stepsisters' feet are too sore from being forced into the slipper for the stepsisters to dance at the ball. I thought they deserved just a little bit of punishment for being so terrible to poor Cinderella!

Perrault considered the moral of the story to be that beauty is a rare treasure, but kindness and courtesy are priceless. Without them, nothing is possible; with them, you can do anything.

And there is another moral: Intelligence, courage, and common sense are also handy, but if all else fails, it helps to have the blessing of a loving godmother! —S.L.T.

Once upon a time,

a rich merchant lived with his daughter. He loved the girl for her beautiful face and her sweet heart. But after his wife died, he decided to marry a second time, and his new wife was selfish and cruel. She had two daughters of her own who were just like her.

The stepmother forced her stepdaughter to wash the pots and pans, scrub the floors, and tend the fire.

The poor girl did not even have a bed of her own, but lay by the hearth every night and rose in the morning covered with cinders. And so her stepsisters called her "Cinderella."

One day the king sent word that he would hold a grand ball. There, the prince would choose a wife.

"I shall wear my red velvet with the lace!" declared the older stepsister.

"I'll wear my satin with the golden flowers!" said the younger one.

Cinderella gathered up her courage to ask a question.

"Can't I—," she said.

"Hand me my stockings," said the older stepsister.

"May I—," said Cinderella.

"Tie this ribbon in my hair," said the younger stepsister.

"Please, can I go to the ball?" asked Cinderella.

"Certainly not!" said her stepmother. And the stepmother and stepsisters swept off in their carriage to the castle, leaving Cinderella alone.

Cinderella sat by the fire. A gentle voice asked, "Why are you crying?"

Cinderella jumped up. There in the kitchen stood a woman with the kindest face she had ever seen.

"Don't worry, my dear," the woman said. "I am your fairy godmother, and I will send you to the ball!"

"But, Godmother," said Cinderella, "I have no carriage or horses or even a gown to wear!"

"Never fear," said her godmother. "And bring me a pumpkin from the garden."

Bewildered, Cinderella picked a plump orange pumpkin.

The godmother touched the pumpkin with the magic
of her wand . . .

. . . and it turned into an elegant coach. The magic turned six mice into six prancing horses, two lizards into two proud footmen, and a rat into a plump coachman.

When the wand brushed Cinderella's rags, she was dressed in pale blue velvet and silver satin. On her feet were a pair of glass slippers, delicate as icicles.

"You are dressed like a queen!" said her godmother. "Behave like one as well. Be kind and courteous to all you meet. And leave the ball before midnight, or everything that my spells have created will vanish."

Cinderella promised to come home by midnight and rode off to the ball.

When Cinderella walked into the ballroom, the fiddlers paused on their strings. The dancers craned their necks to see her. The prince bowed low and asked her to dance.

Whispers raced through the crowd.

"She must be a princess from some foreign land."

"How gracefully she dances!"

"What a sweet smile!"

"Why, the prince can't keep his eyes off her!"

But Cinderella remembered her godmother's words.

Before midnight, she curtsied to the prince and hurried out the door.

Just as Cinderella's coach rolled up in front of her house, the church clock struck twelve times. Cinderella found herself in rags once more, sitting on a pumpkin, with mice and lizards and a big rat at her feet.

The next night, the king held another ball. Cinderella's godmother sent her in a gown of white silk sparkling with diamonds and the same glass slippers. The prince danced with no one else.

"But please," he begged, "won't you tell me your name?"

Cinderella hesitated. And the clock struck the first stroke of midnight.

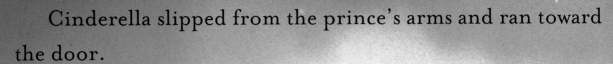

Cinderella slipped from the prince's arms and ran toward the door.

"Wait!" he cried, running after her. But when he looked outside, the beautiful princess was nowhere to be found. He could see nothing but a shabby little servant girl with a pumpkin in her arms.

On the steps was one of the glass slippers.

When Cinderella's stepsisters arrived home, they were full of stories about the mysterious princess.

"The prince swears he'll bring that slipper to every home in the kingdom!" exclaimed the younger stepsister. "And he'll marry the woman whose foot fits into it!"

"Well," said the elder one, "that woman will be me!"

"No," said the younger, "me!"

The next day the prince arrived. A servant followed him, carrying the glass slipper.

The elder stepsister sat on a stool. She shoved and pushed until she cried. But she could not get her foot into the shoe.

The younger stepsister tried next. She wiggled and twisted until she sobbed. But her foot would not fit either.

Then the prince heard a quiet voice asking, "May I try, too?"

"Get back to your kitchen!" cried the stepmother.

But the prince remembered Cinderella's voice and her gentle eyes and her sweet smile. He knelt and slipped the shoe on Cinderella's foot. He was not surprised when she drew the matching slipper from her pocket and placed it on her other foot.

"*You* are the princess I danced with!" he said. "I knew it the minute I saw you!"

Cinderella and the prince were married as soon as the wedding feast could be prepared. And Cinderella, who was as good as she was beautiful, invited her stepsisters and her stepmother to the wedding. Her stepmother was too out of sorts to dance, and as for the stepsisters, their feet were too sore from trying on the slipper. It was weeks before they had recovered enough to dance even a jig.

But Cinderella and her prince lived happily ever after.